Disney's
Winnie the Pooh
Believe in Yourself

It can be kind of scary,

Trying something new.

Just remember

You can do it.

Just believe in you!

Piglet hummed cheerfully as he finished sweeping his front step. He was rather enjoying himself, as he often did when he was busy tidying up his house. It was a comfortable sort of thing to do.

Just then a very excited Roo hopped into view.
"Hello, Piglet!" Roo shouted. "We're going on a picnic! Pooh is coming. And Tigger. And Rabbit and Eeyore. Would you like to come, too?"

"Oh, yes! This is just the right sort of day for a picnic!" Piglet exclaimed. "Wait for me, Roo! I'll just get the haycorn cookies I baked this morning."

"We're going to the big meadow!" Roo told Piglet as they set off to join the others. "Mama says there are flowers and butterflies and soft places to sit!"

It all sounded wonderful to Piglet.

"Here you are, Buddy Boys!" Tigger cried when Piglet and Roo met up with their friends.

"And right across that stream is our perfect-for-a-picnic meadow." Pooh said.

Piglet looked at where Pooh was pointing. Then he looked at the stream. They had to cross over a log to get to the other side! Suddenly Piglet wasn't feeling so happy anymore.

"C'mon, everybody" Tigger called. "Follow me!"
Tigger bounced across the log, chattering to Pooh. Pooh
crossed—balancing a honey pot in each hand.

Roo jumped into his mother's pouch, and they crossed together. Eeyore ambled slowly across with a picnic basket in his mouth.

"Can we speed things up here?" Rabbit muttered from the rear.

Soon only Piglet was left.

"Oh, dear!" cried Piglet. "I can't do it. I'm much too afraid to cross."

"You are kinda small for this sort of thing, aren't you, Little Buddy?" Tigger said. "Too bad."

"What are we waiting for?" Rabbit asked. "Let's get hopping."

"We can't go without Piglet," Pooh said.

Piglet felt terrible. He didn't want to miss the picnic. But he also didn't want to cross that log.

"It's too hard for me, Pooh," Piglet said. "I just don't think I can do it."

"But Piglet," Pooh said, "you've done hard things before."

"I have?" Piglet asked, surprised.

"Oh, yes," Pooh said very definitely.

"Remember when you were sleeping over at my house, and Owl came to tell us there were shooting stars outside?" Pooh asked.

"I remember," Piglet said. "It was very dark, and I was afraid to go out."

"You were afraid, but you went outside to look at the stars anyway," Pooh said.

"I did, didn't I?" Piglet said. "And it was wonderful!"

Piglet felt a little better. He stood up a little straighter.
"Thank you for reminding me of that, Pooh," he said.
"You're welcome, Piglet," Pooh said.

"Hey—and wasn't that you who saved Roo from the bees, Piglet?" Tigger asked. "That was splendiferous!"

"Yes, yes, that was me," Piglet said.

"Aren't you scared of bees, Piglet?" Rabbit asked. "They sting, you know."

"Yes, I know," Piglet said. "And I was scared. But Roo needed my help."

"You were very brave, dear," Kanga said gratefully.

"I was?" Piglet asked. He was feeling better and better!

"I was brave once, too!" Roo said. "Remember, Piglet? We were brave together."

Piglet didn't remember.
"It was at the sack race at my birthday party," said Roo.

"Oh, yes! Now I remember," Piglet replied. "Everybody said we were too small to be in the race. And we were afraid they might be right."

"But we showed them!" Roo shouted. "We even won!"

"We sure did!" Piglet laughed. Piglet wondered how he could have forgotten. He had felt so proud that day.

"See, Piglet?" Pooh said. "You've done lots of things you didn't think you could do."

"Yeah!" said Tigger. "You're downright couragerous!"

Piglet took a deep breath. He looked at the log. Then he looked at his friends.

"This is hard, but if I try, I think maybe I can do it," he said.

Piglet stepped onto the log. He was still scared. But he crossed the log anyway—one careful step at a time.

When Piglet had made it across the stream, his friends all cheered. "We knew you could do it!" Pooh said.

"And now *I* know I can do it, too," Piglet said happily. "I just had to remember to believe in myself!"

A LESSON A DAY
POOH'S WAY

Believe in yourself

And you can do

Great things!